THE
LITTLE HOUSE
BY THE
SEA

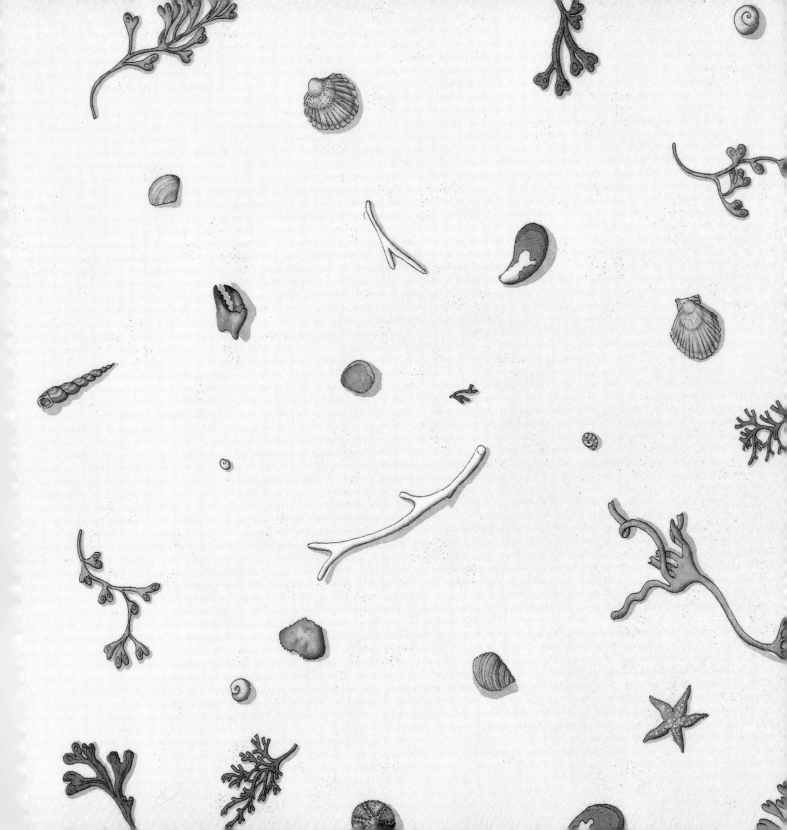

For John and Anne Forrester

A Red Fox Book

Published by Random House Children's Books
20 Vauxhall Bridge Road, London SW1V 2SA

A division of Random House UK Ltd
London Melbourne Sydney Auckland
Johannesburg and agencies throughout the world

© Benedict Blathwayt 1992

First published by Julia MacRae Books 1992

Red Fox edition 1994

3 5 7 9 10 8 6 4

Printed in Singapore

RANDOM HOUSE UK Limited Reg. No. 954009

THE LITTLE HOUSE

BY THE

SEA

~BENEDICT~
BLATHWAYT

Red Fox

Once there was a little house by the sea.

Its door was gone and its windows were empty.

It belonged to nobody.

But mice lived snug and dry in the rough
stone walls.

Rabbits nibbled sweet weeds in the overgrown garden.

Sheep sheltered from the rain in the doorway.

Sparrows flew in and out of the broken windows
and nested in the roof.

A stray cat came to sleep in the fireplace.

And a seagull liked to perch high on the
chimney stack.

One day somebody else came to the little house...

... and began to change everything.

He mended the roof and made a new door.

He fitted new windows.

He filled in the gaps in the wall,
and dug the garden.

And then he lit a fire in the fireplace.

Now he lived in the little house. It was neat and
tidy and warm and cosy ...

... but he was all alone.

So he put milk out for the cat.

He made the sparrows welcome.

He let the sheep shelter in the shed and pretended
not to see the rabbits in the garden.

He did not mind when the mice found
a new crack in the wall.

Even the seagull was happy. The little house
by the sea had a place for everyone.

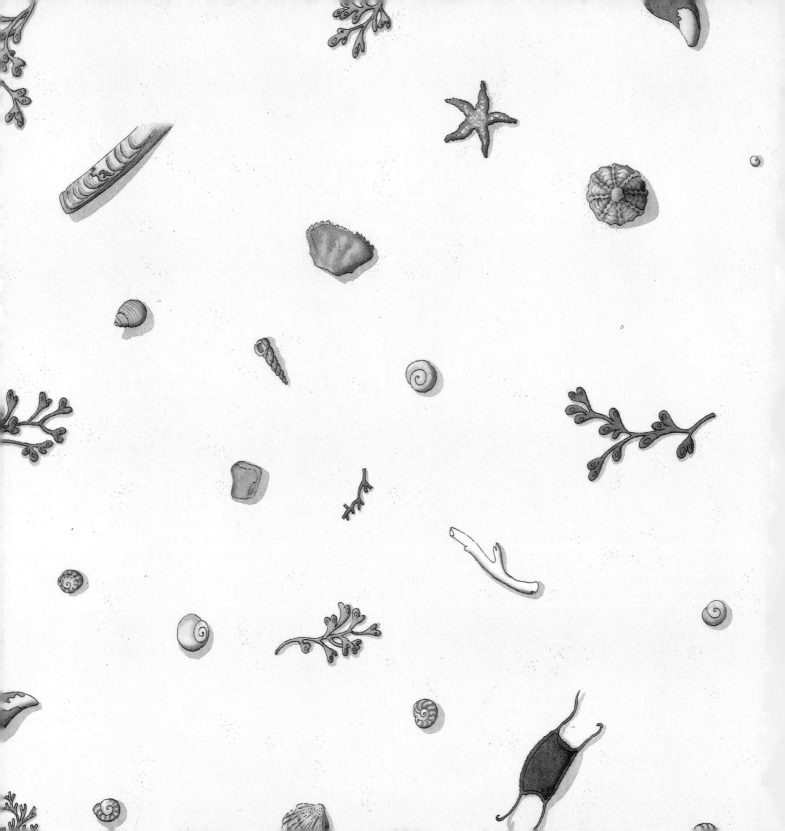

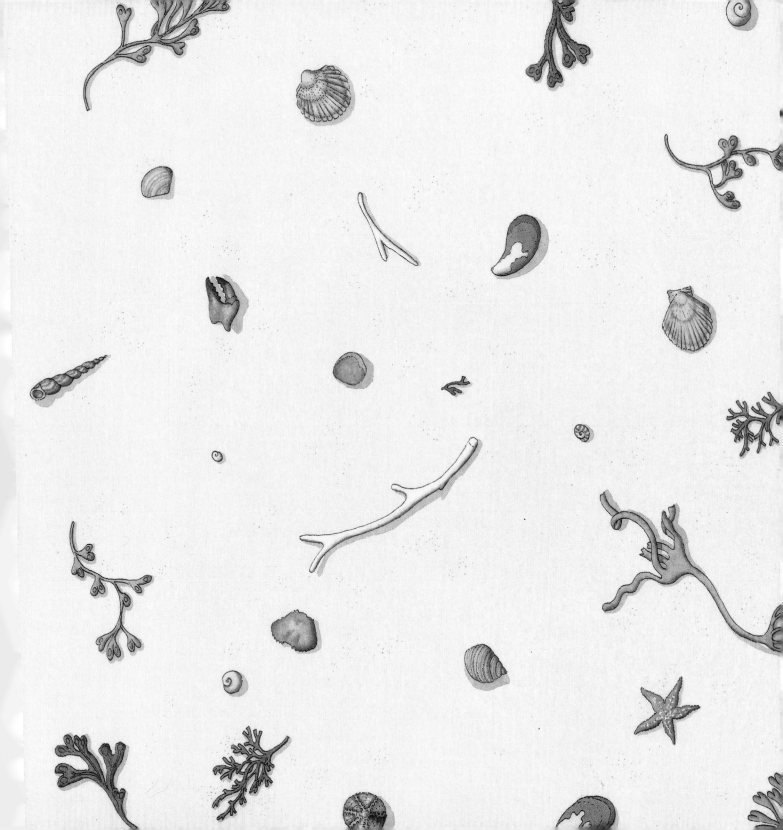